North Sea or Wadden Sea?

Bibliographic information of the German National Library: The German National Library records this publication in the German National Bibliography; Detailed bibliographic data is available on the Internet via dnb.dnb.de.

© 2019 James Watt

Manufacturing and Publishing:

BoD – Books on Demand, Norderstedt.

ISBN: 9783735782595

The Lugworm

As is often the case, dense fog reigned. It was so foggy you didn't even see your hand in front of you.

The sunrise could possibly be guessed by the brightness, but the whole area was wrapped in a deep, pale grey.

It was windless and otherwise quiet. Just quiet, extremely quiet and quiet. The fog just didn't want to give way.

Between the toes, the fine but fog-damp sand quoll out, which accumulated underfoot as it walked slowly across the beach.

Was there still on the beach or somewhere in the mudflats?

Step by step, Hannes – walked very slowly – through the thick fog.

A seagull called from a very far away, but no one should answer it. The other seagulls have apparently stayed on the ground because of the dense fog, rather than

becoming animal.

"Oops!" Whispered Hannes, ... " What was that? "

Right next to him, something cracked without him even beginning to see what was happening around him.

That's when the saying known for such occasions occurred to him: "As you can see, you don't see anything!"

And so it was. The cracking was over and there was stillness again.

What is supposed to ...?!, Hannes thought and went slowly, step by step. Suddenly there was something.

His gaze lowered down to the sandy ground. What!?!

Nothing but mudflat. Just below his feet is much sand. So quite heavy, such wet sand.

But how did he suddenly get into the middle of the mudflats? He hadn't seen anything through the fog, but he thought he was much further back on the beach.

A few inches in front of him, a mysterious thing snaked upward from the sand. "What is this?" Hannes wondered because he could not immediately accurately recognize the deformations on the ground because of the dense fog.

Yeah, there he was! A little greeting from the lugworm.

But what now? What to conclude from this and, above all, what direction did Hannes have to go again in order to get back to the beach?

... The squiggle of the lugworm, after all, did not indicate an exact direction.

Eventually, Hannes decided to seek another lugworm from whose legacies he might be hoping for an answer to his question about direction.

Whacked! Because right in the immediate vicinity apparently another lugworm lived.

But like many of his peers, he was offended because of the weather and the low tide and stuck his head in the sand, as was the rest of his body.

But even this worm could not give Hannes any indication of the direction of the path home ...

"When is the stupid fog finally going to disappear?!" He cursed, going from one lugworm to the next. No one could answer him the question of the safe way back to the mainland.

So the hours passed, and the tough, impenetrable fog continued to lie over the mudflat like a dense veil.

It was still windless, so it seemed the fog stays there all day and just doesn't disappears.

Somewhere nearby, a dull engine noise could be felt ... But where did it come from?

From which direction? And from where did it seem to move?

The buzz of the diesel engine got louder and louder. "Somewhere it has to come from ...!?!," Hannes thought, searching in the thick fog in vain for traces of outlines that could even begin to give him a way to recognize a vehicle.

"Wait a minute ... A vehicle? "Wondered Hannes? "That can't be the case!" At that moment he saw a large, dark surface appear in the fog.

"This can't possibly be a vehicle!" He thought to himself, trying to spot further outlines of the great shadow.

The horizon darkened noticeably, the fog also grew darker. "What is that just ...?" Cursed Hannes.

"Oh oh ... That can't be true! "He thought, barely trusting his eyes.

Over the last few hours, Hannes has lost his way in the mudflats due to the dense fog and poor visibility that he had now walked far towards the open sea and it is only a few meters to the fairway. And in it the large container ships, which are sometimes almost 400 meters tall and enormous.

And now something like that ...

A large, dark house wall seemed to accommodate him.

No, no house wall ... An entire skyscraper, a house complex. A small town ...

Only a few meters separated Hannes ' footpath from the fairway, and so immediately in front of him this huge ship appeared.

It pushed a big wave in front of it, so Hannes had to pick up his legs to avoid being washed away.

Running, kind of running, it was now said, and that as fast as it gets. Because the bow wave of such a large ship is not entirely harmless, even if the container giant does not drive its usual cruising speed in this area.

Hannes galloped like a wild horse over the mudflats and very often came dangerously close to the mudflat inhabitants ...

Many lugworms buried deeper into the mudflat to avoid becoming wider and flatter through the firm, stomping steps. The mudflat dwellers eventually feel every little shock.

And when such a fully-grown person approaches with nimble steps, you may get a lugworm a headache.

Normally, there is also no "lugworm pharmacy" available in the mudflat, so that the poor lugworms are on their own and in such a case have no way of getting appropriate headache remedies.

The bow wave of the container giant was getting closer and closer and gradually crawled out of the fairway at great speed.

The lugworms didn't care, because they have long been familiar with this phenomenon and grew up with it.

But Hannes slowly got panicked anxiety because he saw absolutely nothing in the thick fog and ran haphazardly through the area. He could not have guessed a direction of the sky or a saving stretch of riverside and continued to hear the dull hum of the large, very large ship's house, which was getting closer and closer to it.

Meanwhile, the flood also made him create, because the water was now coming towards him from all sides. The mudflat sank into zero command, and any navigation had now become enormously difficult for Hannes.

After a felt eternity of haphazard wandering around, Hannes suddenly fell up to his neck into a priel from which he was difficult to free himself under his own power.

All the shouts and screams didn't help, you didn't hear him ...

Gradually, in the seemingly untoo-long minutes of his not too long life, Hannes seemed almost entirely exhausted and confused, recalling the admonishing words of an old mudflat-leader.

Hikes in and through the mudflats were well known to him, but today the fog made a dash for him through the bill.

Instead of going back to the saving shore, Hannes made many new acquaintances, such as those with the lugworms, the shells and other mudflats. He also heard seagulls calling, but he didn't see them.

His mobile phone became unusable when he fell into the priel to his chagrin, so he could not request help along the way. So Hannes probably or badly had to pull himself together and look for a way that gets him out of the danger zone as quickly as possible.

After quite a while, a quiet hum approached from very far away ...

The container steamer had, thankfully, somehow continued and didn't bother any more. But there was a new engine noise that Hannes could only faintly take from the depths of the fog.

Completely exhausted and soaked to the skin of salt water, he continued to trudge through the rising water and heard the engine noise come ever closer to him.

It was a water guard lifeboat. Hannes was reported missing by acquaintances on land.

Overjoyed and close to powerlessness, Hannes was hoisted into the boat.

The next morning then the big puzzle ...

Did Hannes just dream everything, or was it really?

The answer is certainly known only to the lugworm.

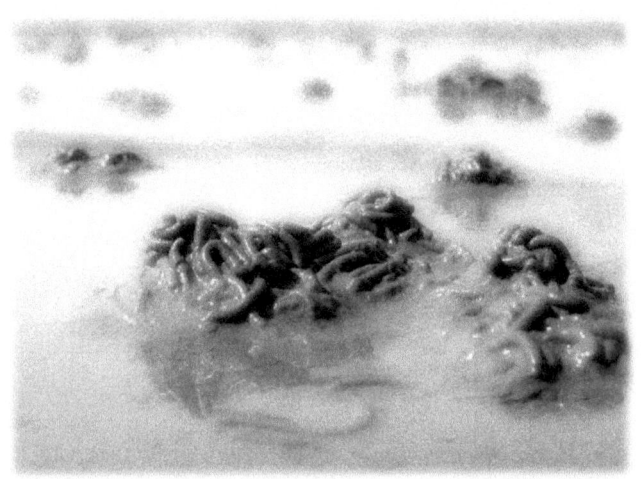